The Light in Lost and Found

Written by T. K. Spencer

Illustrated by Jenna Elluzzi

First published 2026

ISBN: 979-8-9949636-0-9 (hardcover)
ISBN: 979-8-9949636-1-6 (paperback)

Published by TKS Publishing
Windham, NH

Printed in the United States of America

to everyone reading this, shine

In the woods a boy sat,
huddled amongst the shadows and leaves and limbs.

He wasn't lost and he wasn't afraid. He was alone but he wasn't lonely. He was content in his solitude.

Perfectly content sitting in the silence of the night, he sat and stared up beyond the reach of the trees, where the stars shone for anyone who took the time to look.

He liked to believe they shone a bit more for him, those stars, as he smiled into the dusky heavens where they nestled, resting peacefully, amongst the twinkling and the twilight; as they smiled down on him resting peacefully among the timber and the trees, legs crossed, hands palm to palm in his lap.

He held something there, between his hands; something dear and warm and all his own. A shine shimmered out with every shift of his hands, little bits of light peeking out between his fingers, blinking in and out, startling the darkened stillness around him with a diffused, albeit temporary, glow.

It was this glow and a glance, this sudden glimmer, that brought a girl to the edge of the wood.

There she was, this solitary stranger, peering into the shadows of pine and poplar, curious and confused by the brief brilliance breaking through the trees onto the path where she stood. The light cast her shadow on the ground behind her, away from the wood and toward the safety of the familiar, her familiar.

Truth be told, she never noticed it until now, this copse at the edge of nothing, this wood. Head down and unfocused, her absent wanderings lead her here; she knew she had never been into this forest. Perchance it was happenstance, but whatever it was that caught her attention, it was the light that kept it, that lit the path that led her here, that invited her in.

Shoulders back and face impassive, she held her breath for a moment and, tucking a loose strand of long dark hair behind her ear, she stepped into the darkened wood, only pausing between the brief flashes and the immediate darkness, to find her way.

He sat in the middle of the wood in a clearing all his own. The boy stared at the stars above, all the while absentmindedly opening and closing his hands around the light he held, feeling the warmth from the glow.

She followed that wisp of light blinking through the trees, breaking through the darkness, off and on, and it led her to a clearing in the wood, into an opening in the trees exposed to the starry night sky, and to a solitary boy sitting comfortably in the middle of it all, staring wistfully into the dotted darkness above him.

The boy smiled as he watched the stars dance within the darkness above him. He watched as they lit, luminescent, between the leaves. He watched as they blinked at him curiously from within the trees.

He tilted his head to one side, confused. As familiar as he was with the stars above, he had never encountered them out of their space and into his; and, as much as they twinkled, he never knew them to blink.

He was familiar with their shine, though, and these stars shone as bright as any he had seen before.

He stared curiously at those stars and they stared back until shifting their light to the light in his hands. He looked down at his hands, returned his gaze to those two stars, and opened his hands slowly, revealing the pulsating light within. It pushed the night away and with it the mystery before him.

The boy saw a girl.

He smiled.

She did not.

She stared back, an eyebrow arched in consternation and confusion, at this boy sitting alone in the woods smiling up at her; at this smiling boy with star light in his hands.

"What are you doing?" she started before he could say a word. "Sitting alone in the woods?" she continued, her courage bolstered with curiosity.

"Why are you sitting here alone in the woods?" she echoed herself.

She took a breath in and, pointing, asked, "And what are you holding?".

Again, the light in her eyes met the light in his hands.

"You asked a lot of questions," he chuckled.

She crossed her arms and pursed her lips. She wasn't amused with his laughter and her mood was reflected in the dimming of her light.

Still smiling, he answered.

"I don't remember when I started coming here. I wasn't paying attention and found myself in the woods. I looked up and saw the stars shining down on me and I kept coming back to sit and watch the stars shine. I like to believe they shine for me, but I know anyone willing to look up will see what I see. Maybe some people don't see them, or they only see some but not others. Maybe a few do just shine for me. I'm not entirely sure, but I enjoy their shine all the same."

"And that," she continued, walking into the clearing, walking a bit closer to him. "What are you holding?"

The boy stared at the girl with starlight in her eyes. He spent so long looking up at all the beauty overhead that he never considered how he would be if that beauty looked back at him.

He blinked at the stars in her eyes. She narrowed hers.

He looked down at his hands. He often forgot what he held, what he absentmindedly rolled back and forth between them throughout the night, as he sat in the woods alone with the stars and the sky. It was so much a part of him now that he rarely gave it any thought at all; but how odd it must look, holding light. "This," he began, but stopped. He never thought about it, this light. It was just simply here and his, like he's had it all along.

Her hands made their way to her hips and her stance was nothing less than polite impatience.

For some reason this made him smile even more.

"I don't know. One moment I was watching the stars and the next I was holding one. It feels like it's always been here with me, though. Somehow it's been with me all along or it hasn't or I forgot." He looked uncomfortable with his answer. He meant to ask her about her light but felt embarrassed about his own now. He closed his hands, dimming the clearing.

Hesitantly she stepped closer and, still wary of the light he held, knelt before the seated boy.

He opened his hands slightly and she peered at the light within. They both sat in each other's silence, in their glow, before she abruptly stood up and walked back into the safety of the darkness. She mumbled over her shoulder that she needed to go and quickly retreated back into the woods, stumbling her way through the darkness.

He watched her stand and quickly go back into the woods. He stared into the darkness which swallowed her so completely and heard her crashing amongst the brush. It took a few breaths, a heartbeat, until he realized she had no way of finding her way out, the shadows being so complete.

He entered where she disappeared and slowly opened his hands in the direction of her stumbling, intending to light her way; but he tripped over a root and stumbled himself, losing his footing, his balance, and his light.

She came to a halt as light surrounded her and, turning, found herself face to face with a small glowing orb, a star.

His star.

She absentmindedly lifted her fingers to it but stopped short from touching it.

That felt, somehow, too personal; an intrusion.

She closed her eyes and basked in the glow for only a moment before turning away from him, from it, to the darkness beyond her. His light unveiled the path to the entrance of the woods. Glancing briefly over her shoulder at the boy, she smiled slightly, and followed the path out.

He watched her step from the forest.

His light bobbed briefly at the edge before lazily floating back to his waiting hands.

She turned back to him once she was free of the woods and, shaking her head slightly, quietly said, “I don’t belong in there.” She almost uttered an apology but smiled awkwardly instead and walked hurriedly away from the woods, the light, and him.

His light flashed once more and went dim.

She walked beyond his fading light and into the darkness beyond.

He stared into it, into the nothing, and waited a moment more before turning away from the path, from the dark, and her.

She took a few more steps before turning and calling into the shadows, “It was nice to meet you.” A glow of light flashed from the trees, and his ball of light bobbed at the edge of the woods again. The boy, stumbling as he tried to catch it, replied with a smile, “You, too.”

She had no intention to linger, but she did. She lingered and her lingering brought her closer to the woods again.

They talked.

He looked out from the woods; she looked in. They talked about everything and nothing and all the little bits that fill the spaces between the words. He sat with his back against a tree while she lounged in the grass. The light between them cast shadows into the woods and over the path. It flickered and danced along with their conversation. He asked questions about her and she, in turn, was curious about him. As they spoke his and her wisps of twinkling light

danced between them,

basking them both
in a radiance that

pushed away the night
and the nervousness.

Their conversation continued, easy and flowing, throughout the night. They sat and shared, and their combined glow kept the surrounding night at bay. They talked until their entwined light was subdued by morning's glow and, like a spell broken, the night ended.

As did their conversation.

She sat in confused silence as the morning washed over her, washed away the night, and washed away the protection the darkness offered. There was an intimate warmth as they spent the evening in their own radiance but in the morning sun she felt cold and exposed and raw and vulnerable.

She felt seen and, in being seen, uncomfortable.

"I should go," she said to the boy as she stood and turned away from the woods again. "Thank you, but I shouldn't have stayed so long. I don't belong here. In your woods. It's not," she briefly paused, "for me."

It sounded like a statement to her, but to him a question.

She looked at the woods once more and the boy with whom she spent the evening wrapped in simple, easy conversation. “It was nice talking with you. I don’t know why I came here,” she shrugged. Turning around, she waved to the boy in the woods. She turned around once more and watched him waving back. “This place isn’t for me. I won’t come back,” she whispered to herself as she walked resolutely away from the woods.

She was unsure if she meant it.

The wind carried her whisper to him;
he was sure she did.

Surprisingly to both, she did visit again: the next night, and the next, and the one following that. It got so he found himself waiting for her by the path, joyfully impatient, so he could walk by her side into the woods, toward his clearing.

Their clearing.

It felt like theirs now, he thought, as she huddled up against him, side by side, her head on his shoulder, a soft breeze tickling her hair across his face.

"Do you think that your light came from up there," she nodded to the stars above, "before it was with you? You sounded unsure when I asked you this a few nights ago. Or was it with you the entire time and you didn't realize it until you came to sit here?"

The boy sat in silence for a moment, thoughtful.

"Stars are a funny thing. We think they have been up there forever but we can't see the same stars each night. Sometimes there are more; sometimes less." He paused and looked into his own light. "Maybe mine is similar to those in the night sky; sometimes more, sometimes less, but it's all the same."

He looked skyward and the stars above seemed to sparkle in response.

The boy wanted to ask the girl about her light but something shifted in her, something passed briefly across her face, and her eyes betrayed her thoughts.

It wasn't envy or despair, the boy thought. To him it looked like longing and that look of longing lingered longer in his thoughts than it did in the look she briefly held.

Over the nights, their talks became deeper; their time together, longer; the space between them, closer.

Their stars would often dance between them now and, more often than not, he was unsure whose light was whose when the evening ended.

One night much like the other nights, and also very much unlike any other night, the girl entered the woods but stopped before entering the clearing. She stood at the edge, watching the boy from the protection of the shadows.

The boy's light saw her before he did and floated toward her, as it had for so many nights. She held up her hands, gently, to stop his light from coming closer. His light bobbed in place momentarily before slowly returning to the boy. A look of confusion was caught in its glow.

She smiled shyly at the boy. "You once told me that you didn't know why you came here. Or why you stayed; but I think I do, because I feel it, too.

"Do you come here because it makes you feel safe?" she asked him. "Safe from whatever it is which you need to feel safe?"

He blinked; looked away from her. Focused intently on the ground, he shuffled his feet in the dirt and twigs and sat for a few breaths before answering. "I do feel safe here, like the woods protect me."

She stepped from the shadows into the clearing and sat with him. The boy noticed that her shine was dimmer than usual.

”Safe from what?”
she gently asked.

“If you want,
I will listen.”

The boy sat impassively for a moment and stared into his hands. His light flickered in response to something unsaid. Without looking up from his hands he told her everything that had happened prior to him finding his way into the woods. His light changed with his sharing.

She had only known the calm; had never seen it storm.

It burst brightly, angrily; it wavered warily and shy; it raged around him; hid behind him; it split and spit and showered sparks; it rose high, strained and blinding; it sank low, exhaustingly dim. The boy's shadow, thrown about the copse with jagged and angry angles, stretched long and thin away from him; reaching toward the safe, sheltering shade beyond.

As his sharing grew, his shine lessened. The longer he spoke, the more he darkened, until finally his mood matched the darkness around them.

The boy stopped talking, his breathing quick and shallow. As he recovered so did his light, which nestled gently in his hands again. It shone like before.

“Thank you for sharing you with me,” she said.

“Why did you?”

He smiled warmly at her. “I haven’t felt safe with anyone in a very long time, but now there is you,” he replied.

She smiled but it stopped at her eyes, which seemed to dim even more.

”Are you ok?” he asked, concernedly.

She ignored his question, reached out, and, pulling him to his feet, said,

"Come with me."

The girl and the boy walked slowly through the forest, away from the clearing, toward the edge where the trees met the field; where they had first spoken.

Staring up into the night sky, she asked, "Do you ever feel like it wants to float back into the sky, to join all the other stars twinkling down on us, to shine for everyone to see?"

He paused on the path, among the trees, and watched his light linger between the limbs and leaves.

"Sometimes," he said, "I get the feeling that it wants to be free; but it also wants to stay here," he looked at his hands and then at her, "with me... that it feels safe here with me."

"Your light feels safe with you," she asked gently, "or do you feel safe with it?"

The look he gave her was all the answer she needed.

They continued walking until they reached the edge of woods, where the path wound its way into the fields beyond.

They stood there, hand in hand, beneath the canopy of trees looking out at the vast night sky, looking out at the open, unsheltered field beyond the woods.

He gazed up into the heavens and down at his light. It glowed softly before him. It pulsed differently now.

“I love that you let me see you, truly see you,” she started while staring at the stars above.

“I think the world deserves to see you, too; and I think you deserve to be seen.”

She turned her gaze away from the sky and looked at him.

“You said nights ago that some stars up there,” she looked to the sky again, “might shine for you; and some stars only shine for people who can see them.

“Do you think yours should be up there, too, and given the same chance to shine?”

The boy looked from the girl to the stars above, his eyes filled with apprehension and fear.

"Let it fly away from me? What if I lose it among the stars? I'll be lost in the dark without it."

She released his hand and, stepping into the security of the forest shadows, said softly, "As long as you have you, you won't be in the dark.

"You shine brightly."

The boy, noticing the girl was no longer standing with him, turned toward her voice coming from the darkened woods.

"Why are you leaving? Don't you feel safe with me, too?" he worried.

"I do," she paused, looking into the woods, toward the spot she found him not so many nights ago, "I do feel safe with you but I don't feel safe with so many things. Mostly, I don't feel safe with myself yet. I need that and, perhaps, looking up at those same stars, those stars that helped you feel safe, will do the same for me. I need me again."

"I want to find me," she quietly and cautiously confided. She looked at the boy with a smile on her lips but tears in her eyes, "I don't have me yet and I worry I never will."

"Don't I deserve to shine, too?" she whispered into the woods.

"You need to find your light," the boy whispered, finally understanding. Although he had seen it all along, since her eyes first shined from within the woods, she could not see that same shine. She did not know she had a light all her own; for her there were only shadows.

"And you need to share your shine," she quietly replied, "but only if you are ready. This is a choice only you can make."

The boy slowly looked from the girl to his star to the night sky above and then back to the girl. She smiled at him and this time her smile touched her eyes. They shone, briefly with a burst, more brightly than he had seen before.

With a breath and a sigh, the boy closed his eyes, opened his hands, and let go.

It rose slowly at first, his star, and bathed him in a soft light. Then, in a blink, it was gone.

He did not see where it went, but he had a feeling it was up there, above him, keeping him in its glow. It warmed him knowing that she was right; he hadn't lost his light.

She watched it rise slowly from his hands before splitting in two, one half soaring into the night to twinkle within the twilight and the other half sinking into the boy, leaving an imperceptible line of light between him and his star.

It warmed her knowing she was trusted and he wouldn't be in the dark.

Without saying goodbye, the girl slowly walked into the dark and disappeared from sight.

The boy turned to see her go, to wish her well, to say goodbye, but was met with only shadows and leaves and limbs.

He knew he could go back into the forest to find her but had a feeling she wouldn't be found in the same spot because these were no longer his woods.

It would not be his glade.

These were not his trees and the sky she sat under did not hold the same stars, at least not yet.

He trusted her enough to let go, and so he did.

She trusted him enough to let her go, and so she did.

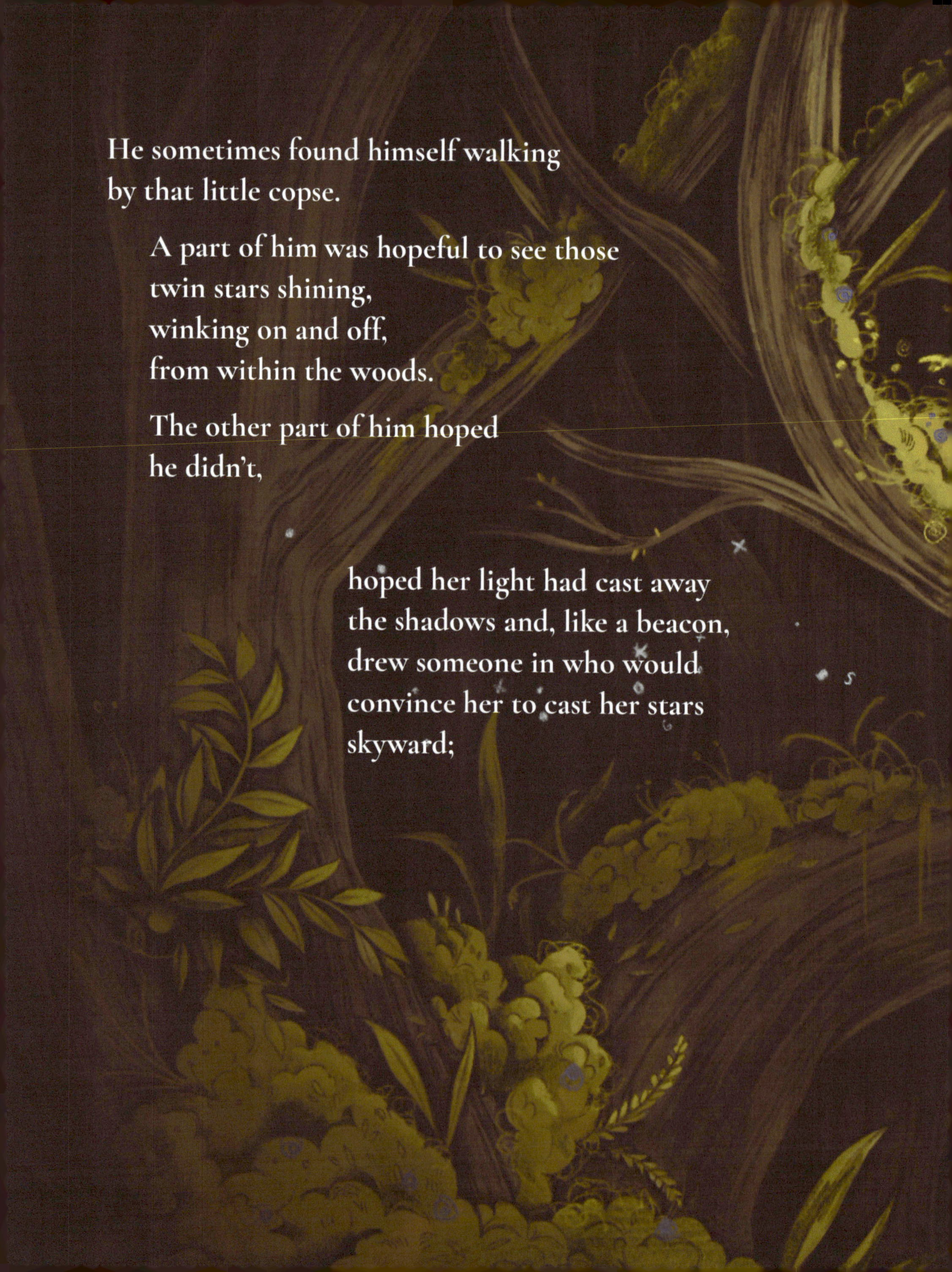

He sometimes found himself walking
by that little copse.

A part of him was hopeful to see those
twin stars shining,
winking on and off,
from within the woods.

The other part of him hoped
he didn't,

hoped her light had cast away
the shadows and, like a beacon,
drew someone in who would
convince her to cast her stars
skyward;

or, better still, she found
she could do it herself.

For who doesn't want to love their light.

Thank You

To my wife, Tiffany, for encouraging me to finish this story and continue working on other stories that I have to tell.

To my yogi friend, Becks, for giving me the space in Shavasana to quiet my mind and unblock all the writing blocks.

To my artist, Jenna, whose illustrative talents gave my story character and color.

And to you, the reader: thank you for opening these pages. I hope you shine brightly.

About the Author

T. K. Spencer lives in New Hampshire with his wife, their three kids, two cats, and one very elderly pup. When he isn't writing, he's out hiking—and when he isn't writing or hiking, he's doing his best impression of a responsible adult. *The Light in Lost and Found* is his debut picture book, written from a simple belief: that everyone carries a light worth sharing.

About the Illustrator

Jenna Elluzzi is an illustrator and surface designer in New York City, where she also studied at Parsons School of Design. Her work takes inspiration from the natural world, old fairy tales and folktales, and woodcut and graphite drawing, and extends a love of all living things.

See more of her work at iizulle.com.

www.ingramcontent.com/pod-product-compliance
Lightning Source LLC
LaVergne TN
LVHW071247210926
848486LV00008B/362